All-Action Animal Art

OVER THE REEF

PowerKiDS press

Juan Calle & William Potter

Published in 2019 by **The Rosen Publishing Group, Inc.**
29 East 21st Street, New York, NY 10010

Cataloging-in-Publication Data

Names: Calle, Juan. | Potter, William.
Title: Over the reef / Juan Calle and William Potter.
Description: New York : PowerKids Press, 2019. | Series: All-action animal art | Includes glossary and index.
Identifiers: ISBN 9781538347447 (pbk.) | ISBN 9781538347461 (library bound) | ISBN 9781538347454 (6pack)
Subjects: LCSH: Marine animals in art--Juvenile literature. | Drawing--Technique--Juvenile literature.
Classification: LCC NC781.C355 2019 | DDC 743.6--dc23

Art by Juan Calle, Color by Luis Suarez (Liberum Donum)
Text by William Potter
Edited by Joe Harris and Sebastian Rydberg, with Julia Adams
Designed by Emma Randall

Manufactured in the United States of America

CPSIA Compliance Information: Batch CWPK19: For Further Information contact Rosen Publishing, New York, New York at 1-800-237-9932.

CONTENTS

GETTING STARTED

THE STEPS

This book shows how you can draw a realistic sea creature starting with simple shapes. You can then add in detail, such as fins, tails, and scales.

WHAT YOU NEED

To follow the steps in this book, all you need is some paper, a pencil (with sharpener), an eraser, paintbrushes, and water-based paint.

The first two steps show the basic building blocks for the body—circles, ovals, and curved lines—and the position of fins.

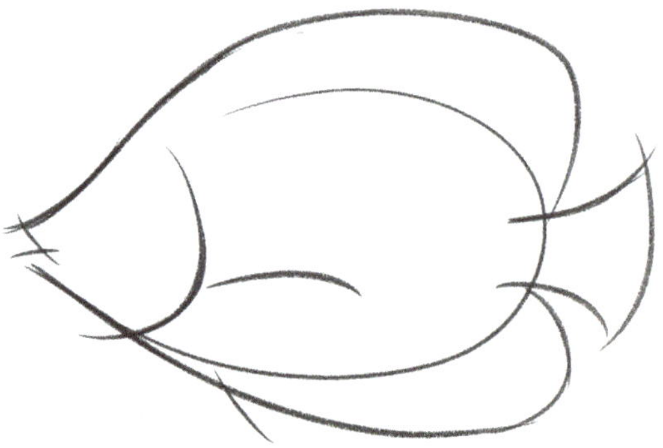

The third step refines these simple shapes and adds detail, such as the eyes and mouth. New lines are in blue as a guide. When you have drawn these outlines, you can erase the working lines you drew in steps 1 and 2.

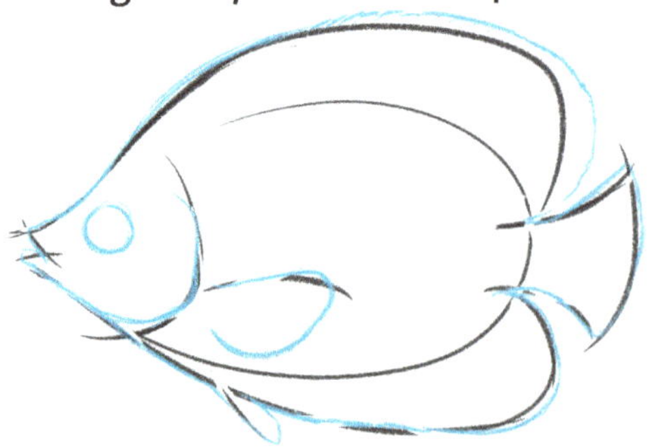

Later steps add extra detail, including gills, teeth, and skin patterns.

The final step is a guide to what shades you should use to complete your picture.

COOL CORALS

Here are a selection of bright corals, sponges, and plants that you can try drawing. Add them to a scene featuring your best reef fish.

Sea fan

Finger coral

Anemone

Tube sponge

Coral reef

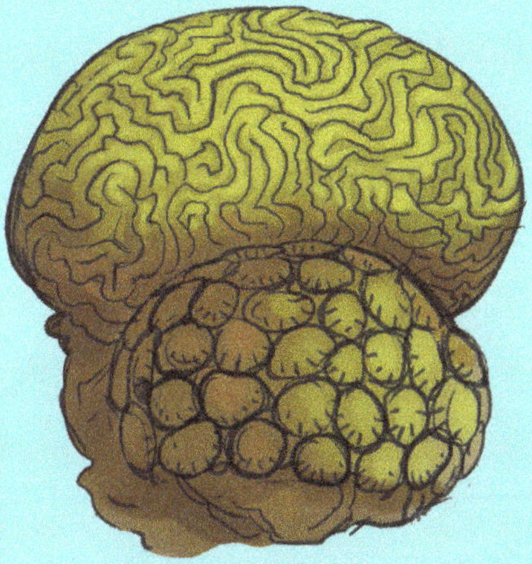

Brain coral

CLOWN FISH

The bright clown fish lives beside an anemone, and is protected by its stings.

1. Begin with a basic fish shape, with a line from head to tail. Mark the head.

2. Add rounded fins. Draw a mouth that curves down at the side.

3. Go over these lines, improving their shapes. Give the fins a slightly bumpy edge, and circle the eye above the mouth.

4. Dot the eye. Add an outline around the mouth, a fan of lines on the fins and tail, and wrinkly lines on the head.

5. Mark the dark stripes on the tail and back fins, plus the three wide, white stripes on the body.

TOP TIP

To create an anemone home for the clown fish, imagine drawing a group of curved worms all reaching up and wriggling in different directions.

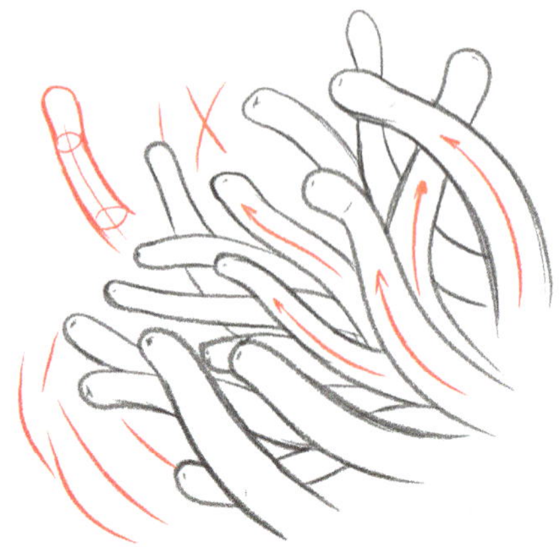

6. The clown fish is bright orange with distinctive white stripes. Add some blue to the shadows on the white areas.

SEAHORSE

This delicate fish uses its curvy tail to cling to reeds and coral branches.

1. Start by drawing a tall, curving body with a long snout, rounded belly, and a spiral tail.

2. Add a fin on the back and another by the head. Use a line to mark where the eye will be.

3. Divide the body into three sections along its length. Draw an eye and the tiny bumps on the head.

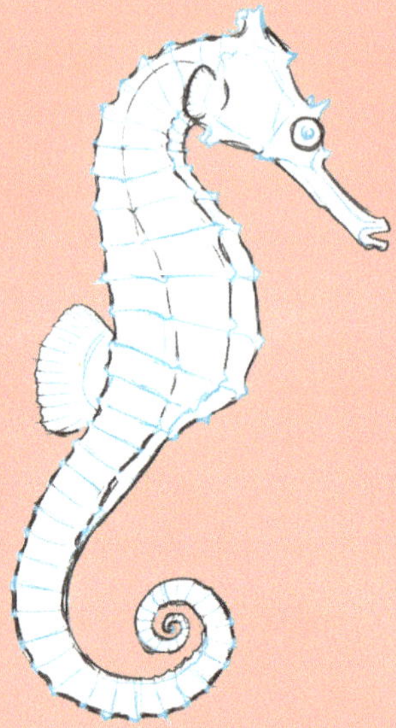

4. Draw lines across the body. Add a small bump where these lines cross the vertical lines and the edge of the body. Add detail to the fins and face.

WILD FACT!

Seahorses pair for life. But it's the male seahorse, not the female, that carries the eggs and gives birth to live young, called fry.

5. Paint this seahorse with yellow shades, adding some pale brown shadows inside each square section on the body.

TOP TIP

The seahorse's bony body appears as a raised grid pattern over its body, with bumps at every corner. Use shadows and highlights to bring out these raised areas.

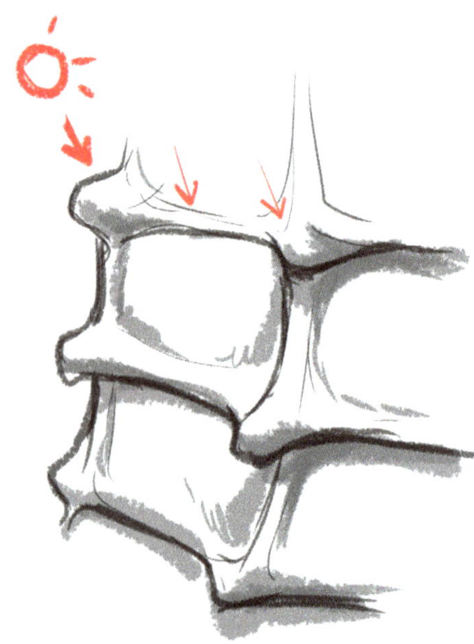

BANNERFISH

This stripy fish has a long, trailing dorsal fin. It likes to live in a large group.

1. Draw a circular body with a pointed mouth. Mark the head position and add an eye.

2. Add one trailing back fin, several rounded fins, and a triangular tail.

3. Add detail around the mouth and eye. Draw fans of lines inside the fins and tail. Place groups of semicircular scales on the body.

4. Carefully mark the dark stripes on the bannerfish's body. The dark stripes cover some of the lower fins.

5. Use a bluish charcoal for the shadows and scales on the fish's body. Paint the stripes in a black wash. The side, back, and tail fins are yellow.

TOP TIP

The bony spines or rays on a fish's fins radiate from the point where they join the body. This is a pelvic fin, usually found on the lower part of the body.

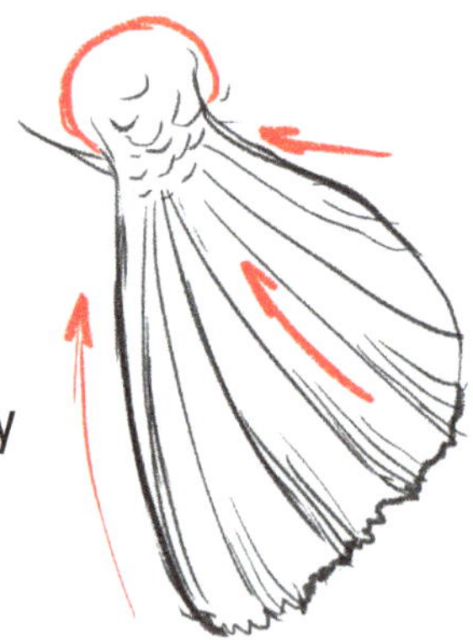

BLUE TANG

This bright fish has a flat body and markings that look like an artist's palette.

1. Start with an oval body joined to a triangular tail.

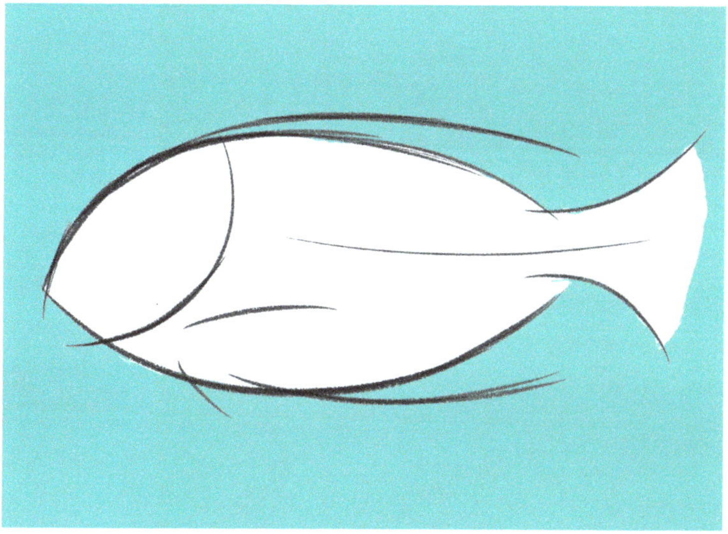

2. Draw the position of the fins and the head.

3. Shape the fins, giving them a rounded edge. Circle the eye, and draw a small mouth on the lower half of the head.

4. Fill the tail and the fins with rows of short lines. Draw a pupil in the eye and the curved lines below the eye.

5. Mark the dark patterns over the blue tang's body, then mark the edges of its upper and lower fins.

6. Paint the blue tang with a blue body and darker blue pattern on the upper half. The tail has a yellow triangle in the middle.

WILD FACT!

The blue tang has sharp spines near its tail. If it is attacked, it thrashes its tail from side to side, inflicting serious injuries.

PUFFER FISH

When in danger, the puffer fish takes in water to inflate into a spiny ball.

1. Start with a circle for the body, and add a line that will help position the mouth and eye.

2. Add two small semicircles to indicate the position of the mouth and side fin.

3. Add the round eye and bottom lip. Draw the rounded fin to the right of the eye.

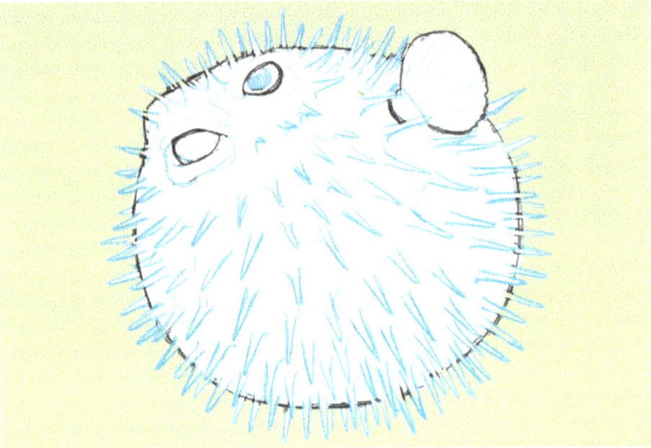

4. Add a pupil in the eye, lips around the mouth, and a fan of lines on the fin. Cover the puffer fish in spines that radiate out from the eye.

TOP TIP

To position the puffer fish spines accurately, draw a series of circles around the body, and draw spines where the circles cross. The spines should point out from the imagined middle of the fish.

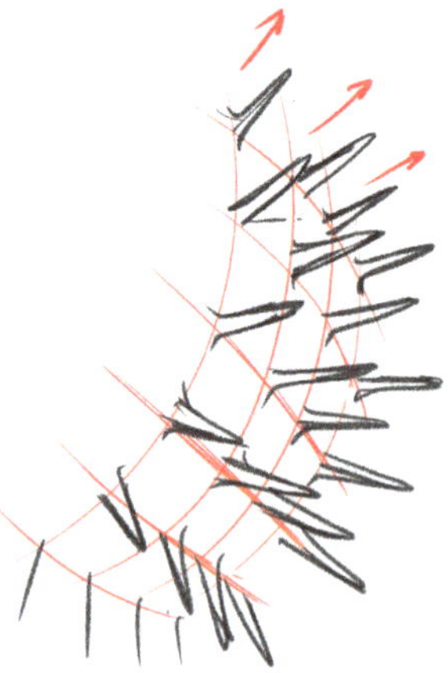

5. Give the fish a pale tan body with a light brown upper edge and a bluish reflection on the lower half. Add shadows below the lower spines.

POTATO GROUPER

This fat-lipped fish has a blotchy pattern and can grow over 6.5 feet (2 m) long.

1. Start with a basic fish shape and draw a line to mark the head.

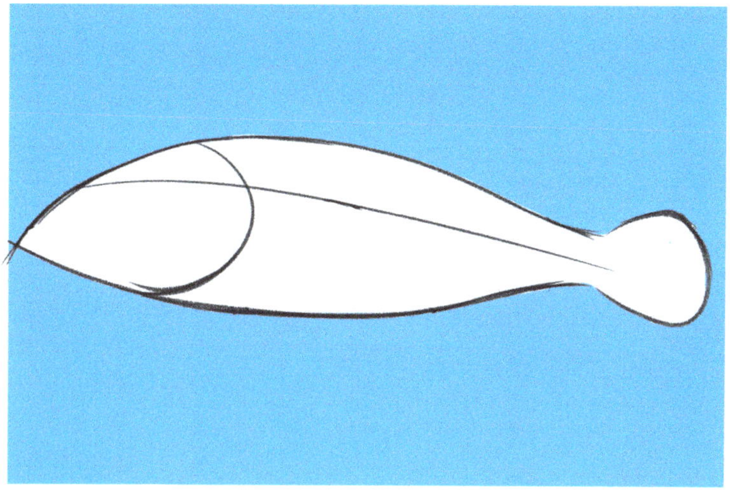

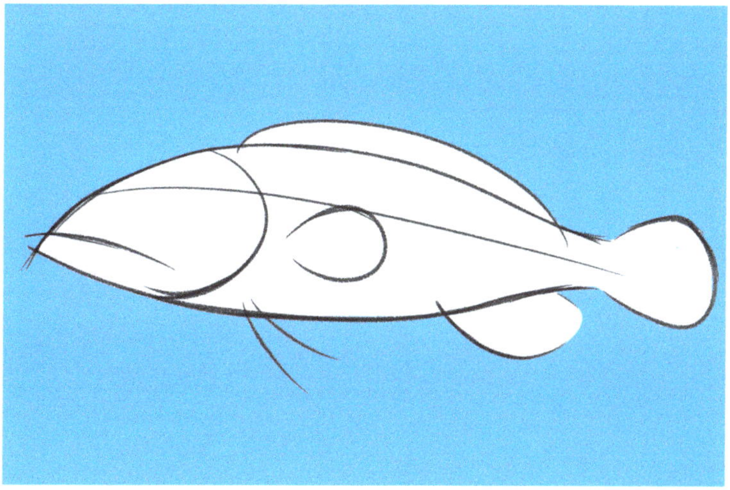

2. Add a wide, downturned mouth and rounded fins.

3. Add curves to the fins. Draw an eye near the front of the head and a slight gap in the mouth.

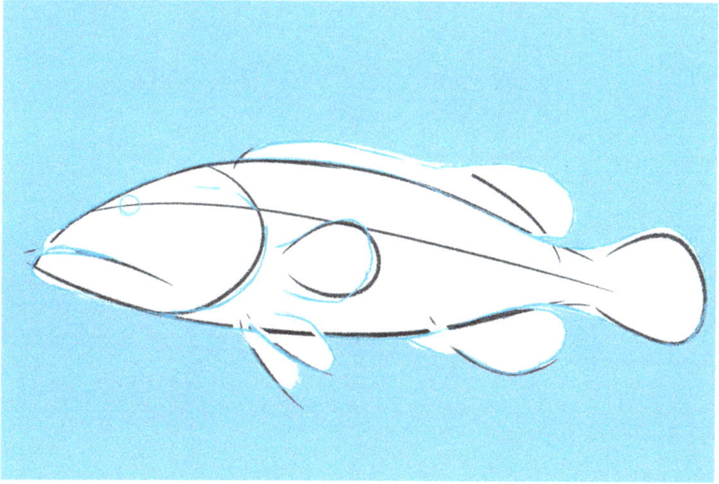

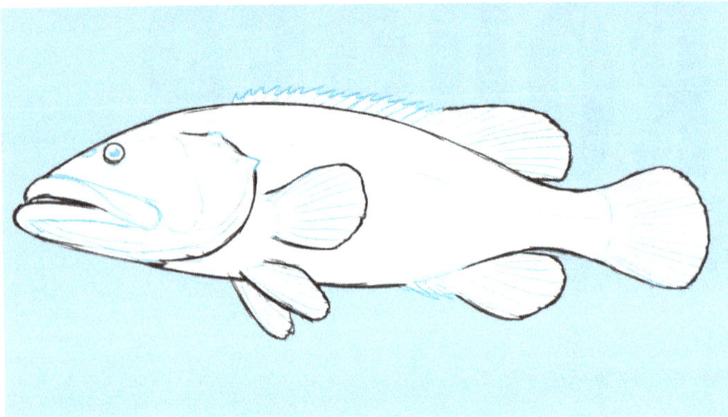

4. Give the fish wide lips and wrinkly lines below the mouth and to the right. Add fans of lines inside each fin and on the tail.

5. Mark the patterns on the grouper's body. It has dashed lines on the face and spots over the body and fins.

6. Paint the grouper's body with a light silver, adding a hint of turquoise to the shadows. The spots and lines on the face are shades of slate.

WILD FACT!
Potato groupers hunt small fish. They catch them by sucking in the surrounding water and eating the fish whole.

GIANT CLAM

Clams have two hard shells they can close to protect their delicate body.

1. Draw an oval with a curved line across the middle.

2. Add a row of bumps over the top and bottom halves.

3. Round off the bumps to form continuous curves. Draw two wavy lines over the dividing line.

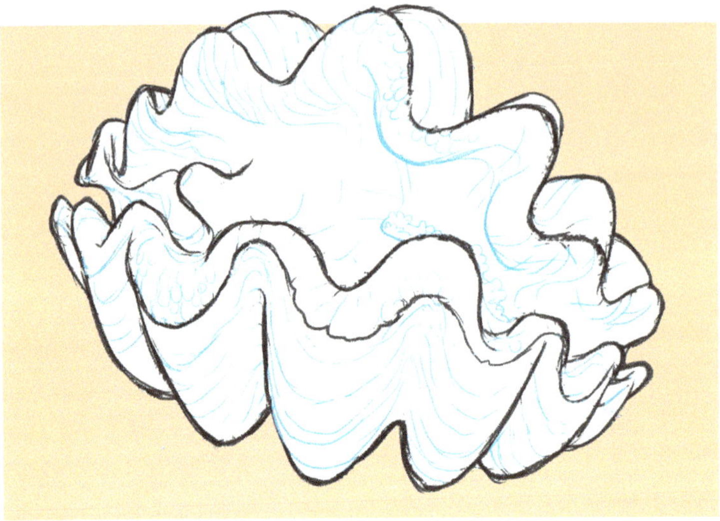

4. Add a series of wavy lines over the outside of the shell halves and wrinkly lines on the inside.

5. The clam's shell is pale charcoal on the outside but full of bright blues and turquoise on the inside, with speckles on the rims.

WILD FACT!

The giant clam can weigh up to a whopping 500 pounds (225 kg). It spends all of its adult life attached to a reef.

TRIGGERFISH

The titan triggerfish is protective of its nest and will chase away intruders.

1. Start with a wide fish shape with a mouth and tail.

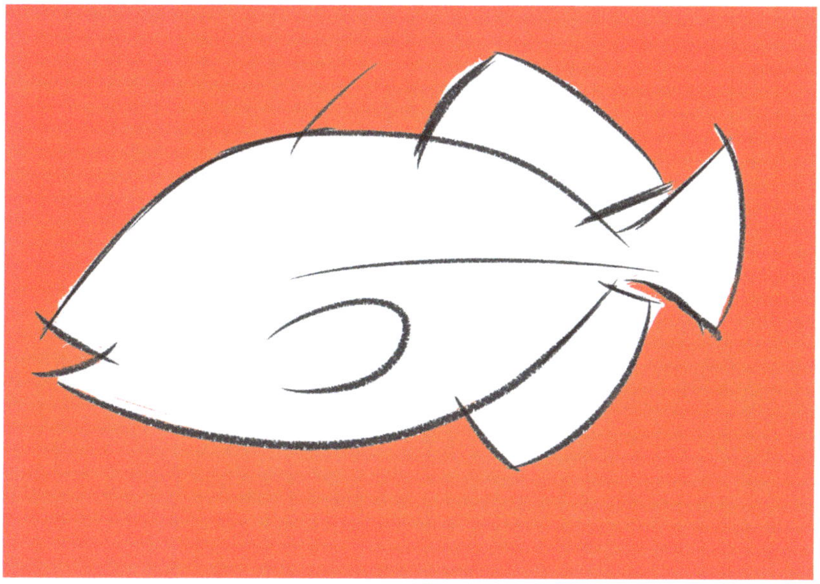

2. Draw the fins at the top and bottom and mark the other fins.

3. Refine the shape of the fins and tail. Add the eye, and shape the open mouth.

4. Add a pupil to the eye and lips around the mouth. Don't forget the teeth! Sketch lines to show the scales on its body.

5. Mark the patterns on the fish. This titan triggerfish has a dark mask, speckles on its scales, and dark fringes to its fins.

6. Paint the triggerfish with a mostly yellow body, adding dark brown patches on the scales and dark blue edges to the fins.

TOP TIP

When painting the diamond pattern of scales, go from dark on the left to a lighter shade on the right, leaving a little space between each diamond.

BUTTERFLY FISH

This bright yellow fish has a shape like the spade from a deck of cards.

1. Draw a heart shape on its side, with a triangular tail on the right.

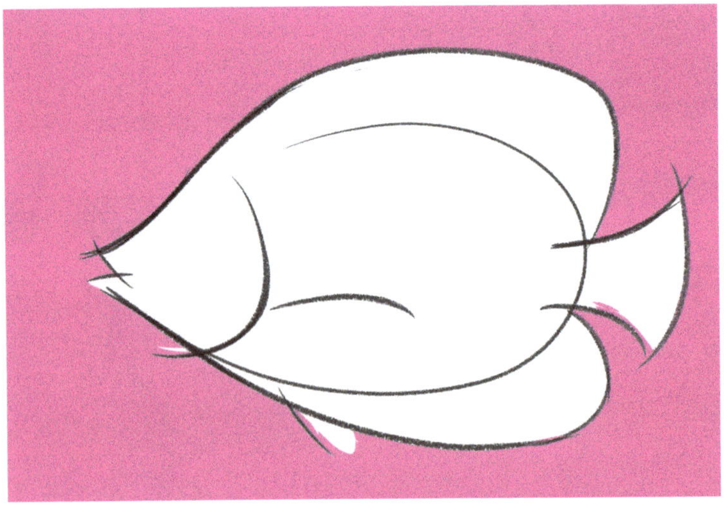

2. Mark the head. The fish has a rounded body and a pointed mouth.

3. Give the fins a rough edge. Draw a large, round eye, curved gill slit, and a side fin.

4. Fill in the pupil of the eye, then add a fan of lines to the fins. Use diagonal lines in two directions to suggest the scales on its body.

5. The butterfly fish has a dark mask patch around its eye, several dark stripes across its body, and a dark fringe to its outer fins.

6. Paint the fish with a bright yellow body, charcoal mask, pale brown diagonal stripes, and thin, deep-blue lines on the fins.

MORAY EEL

This large marine eel hides in crevices waiting to ambush passing prey.

1. Start with two curving lines that form the number "8" on its side. Add an open mouth at one end and a tail at the other.

2. Draw an upper fin along the body length and mark the eel's head.

3. Refine the shape of the long fin, and add a bulge below the head. Draw the open jaw and an eye.

4. Sketch folds where the eel bends, plus a few diagonal lines on the fins. Draw two bumpy nostrils and several sharp teeth in the open mouth.

5. Paint the moray eel with a lime green, adding greenish-blue shadows and a few blotches.

WILD FACT!

Morays are the world's largest eels. They can grow to 13 feet (4 m) long!

LIONFISH

This fish may look attractive, but the spines on its fancy fins are loaded with deadly venom!

1. Start with a basic fish shape, marking the head and mouth.

2. Add a series of curves around the body. This will indicate the positions of the fin rays.

3. Divide the fan shapes around the body into sections to mark individual spines. Draw the round eye.

4. Outline each spine. Draw a fan of lines on the tail fins. Add the growths above the eyes and over the mouth.

5. Lightly mark the zebra-type stripes and spots on the lionfish's body and spines. Use dotted lines on the tail fins.

6. Give the fish a very pale orange skin with rusty red stripes. Alternate wide and thin stripes on the body.

TOP TIP

You can be fairly free when painting the curvy stripes on the fish, filling gaps with thinner stripes. Note that the stripes continue over the eye.

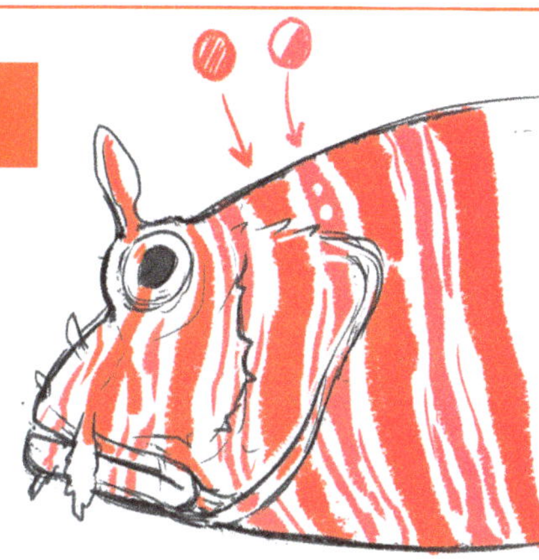

GLOSSARY

ambush A surprise attack from someone waiting in hiding.

blotchy Patchy.

crevice A narrow opening, such as in a rock wall.

delicate Intricate, detailed.

distinctive Singled out as being different and therefore noticed.

dorsal fin The fin of a marine animal that sits on its back.

gill slit One of the many openings of the gills. Animals with gills can breathe underwater.

inflict To cause pain or damage to someone else.

intruder Someone who enters without permission.

palette A thin board on which artists mix their paints.

pelvic fin The fin of a marine animal that often sits behind and below the side (pectoral) fin.

pupil The dark part of the eye that lets light through.

radiate To spread from a central point.

venom Poison that works by injection.

wrinkle A fold or line in something, such as skin.

FURTHER INFORMATION

Books:

Ames, Lee J. *Draw 50 Sea Creatures*. New York, NY: Watson-Guptill, 2017.

Cuddy, Robbin. *Learn to Draw Sea Creatures*. Lake Forest, CA: Walter Foster Publishing, 2015.

DuBosque, Doug. *Draw Animals: Ocean – Rainforest – Desert – Grassland*. Vancouver, WA: Peel Productions, Inc, 2015.

McCurry, Kristen. *How to Draw Incredible Ocean Animals*. North Mankato, MN: Capstone Press, 2013.

Yates, Jane. *I Can Draw Sea Monsters*. New York, NY: PowerKids Press, 2018.

Websites:

PowerKids Press has developed an online list of websites related to the subject of this book. This site is updated regularly. Please use this link to access the list: www.powerkidslinks.com/aaaa/overthereef

INDEX